Enid Blyton

Secret Seven
Fireworks

Illustrated by Derek Lucas

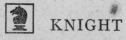

KNIGHT

the paperback division of Brockhampton Press

ISBN 0 340 16285 6

This edition first published 1972 by Knight Books, the
paperback division of Brockhampton Press Ltd, Leicester

First published by Brockhampton Press Ltd 1959
Seventh impression 1971
Text copyright © 1959 Enid Blyton
Illustration copyright © 1972 Brockhampton Press Ltd

Printed and bound in Great Britain by
Cox & Wyman Ltd, London, Reading and Fakenham.

CONTENTS

One

What's happened to the Secret Seven?

PETER, Jack and Janet were walking home from school one fine October day, when someone came skipping up behind them. It was Susie, Jack's sister.

'Hallo, you three!' she said. 'What's happened to the Secret Seven? You never seem to have meetings now.'

'Nothing's happened to the Secret Seven,' said Peter. 'Don't be silly.'

Susie began to chant a little song just behind them.

'The Secret Seven's falling to bits.
It doesn't meet any more.
The only thing that is left of it
Is the silly S.S. on the door!'

'*Susie!* You little horror!' said Jack, angrily. 'Singing like that in the street about the Secret Seven! Falling to bits! You don't know what you're talking about.'

'Oh, I *do*,' said Susie, skipping in front of them now. 'I know you haven't met for ages – I know. Jack's lost his badge – I know you can't use Peter's shed for meeting-places – I know . . .'

Peter, Janet and Jack glared at the smiling, irritating Susie.

'What do you mean – you know we can't use our shed?' demanded Peter. 'You've been snooping.'

'No, I haven't. My ball went over your wall, Peter, and I ran to get it – and I saw your shed full of onions! *Onions!*' Susie laughed loudly. 'So I knew you couldn't be

7

meeting there – and I've a very particular reason for asking if the Secret Seven is still going on or not.'

Peter stopped at once, and the others stopped too. *Now* what was Susie up to? Why was she so anxious to know about the Secret Seven?

'What's this silly, particular reason?' asked Peter, sharply, 'Go on – tell us.'

'Well, you see – if your Secret Seven has stopped, I thought *I'd* like to form a Secret Seven Club of my own,' said Susie, solemnly, with a wicked glint in her bright eyes. 'I thought I'd ask Leonard, and Harry and . . .'

'What! Copy *us*!' said Janet, in scorn. 'Well – *I* wouldn't want to be a copy-cat like that!'

'And anyway, forget about it,' said Peter. 'The Secret Seven is meeting this very Saturday morning. Isn't it, Jack?'

This was the first that Jack had heard of any meeting but he nodded his head vigorously. 'Yes. Let me see – ten o'clock, wasn't it, Peter?'

'That's right,' said Peter, giving Janet a little nudge in case she should say *she* hadn't heard of any meeting.

'It'll be a pretty smelly meeting, sitting on top of all those onions,' said Susie. 'Shall I help you to clear them out of the shed?'

'*No!*' roared Peter and Jack together.

Janet gave Susie a push. 'Go away!' she said, fiercely. 'You're just *trying* to be annoying. Fancy thinking *you* could run a club!'

'I could, easily,' said Susie. 'You just wait and see!'

She skipped off, leaving the other three feeling really furious. 'Can't you possibly keep that sister of yours in order, Jack?' said Peter. 'Like I do Janet?'

'You do *not* keep me in order,' said Janet, at once, and

stalked off ahead of the two boys. They looked at one another.

'*Girls!*' said Jack, in a disgusted voice, low enough for Janet not to hear. 'They're all the same.'

'Except that Susie is a bit worse,' said Peter. 'Now look, Jack, we'd better have this Secret Seven meeting, as we've said we're going to. It's an awful bore, really, because we'll have to turn all those onions out and put them somewhere else. I hope my father won't mind!'

'Well, look, let's all come at a quarter to ten, not ten, and help you,' said Jack. 'We can easily tell the others in good time.'

'All right,' said Peter. 'Quarter to ten, then – and tell Susie if she dares to so much as put her nose round the door of our shed, I'll . . . I'll – well, I really can't think of anything bad enough to do to her.'

'What shall we have a meeting about?' said Jack. 'Nothing much has happened – no mystery or anything to work on. But we must have something to *talk* about.'

'Well, we will,' said Peter, an idea suddenly coming into his head. 'What about planning for Bonfire Night? It will be here in a couple of weeks or so, and we ought to start saving up for fireworks, and decide about a guy – and where to burn him.'

'Golly, yes!' said Jack, thrilled. 'Of course – that's what we'll have the meeting about. If we don't start saving up soon we shan't have any fireworks on Guy Fawkes Night. Jolly good idea of yours, Peter.'

'And for goodness sake find your badge,' said Peter. 'Susie said you'd lost it.'

'What a tell-tale!' said Jack. 'I *had* lost it. It went to the cleaner's on the lapel of my blazer – Mother didn't notice it. And I was awfully upset when the blazer came back without it, and grumbled like anything. That's how Susie knew it was gone.'

'Well, you'd better get your mother to make you a new one,' said Peter. 'Can't have anyone turning up without a badge, you know.'

'All right, all right. Why don't you lose *yours* for once?' said Jack. 'Then you'd know what it feels like. How was *I* to know that my mother was going to send my blazer to the cleaner's all of a sudden?'

Peter gave him a friendly punch. 'Don't be so touchy! Tell George about the meeting on Saturday, will you? And I'll tell Colin. Janet will tell Pam and Barbara.'

'Right,' said Jack, as Peter swung in at the gate. 'There's one good thing to be said for Susie – she's made us call a meeting! I shall look forward to it. So long, Peter!'

'So long!' said Peter, and ran down the path that led to the shed where the Secret Seven met. He opened the door – and a dozen onions rolled out at once. He kicked them back.

'You wait till Saturday!' he said. 'You'll have to get out of here, and make room for the Secret Seven! Janet – Janet! Where are you? I say – won't it be fun to have one of our meetings again!'

Two

Password, please!

ON Saturday morning Janet and Peter were down by their shed, together with two or three barrows of all sizes, ready to wheel away the onions stored there. The gardener hadn't been at all pleased when he heard that his precious onions were to be taken out of the nice dry shed.

'But, Gardener, we asked Dad, and he *said* we could put them into the old summer-house,' said Peter.

'Rain blows in there,' said the gardener.

'Dad said we could take the old tarpaulin sheet and cover them over with that,' said Janet. 'You see, Gardener, this really *is* our shed. We meet here. You know we do.'

'Not for weeks you haven't,' said the gardener. 'Well, I'm busy – you'll have to move the lot yourselves. Take you a good time, too!'

'Oh, there'll be seven of us,' said Peter. 'Many hands make light work, you know.'

'You be careful that too many cooks don't spoil the broth,' said the man, and walked off, his rake over his shoulder.

'That was quite bright of the gardener,' said Janet, astonished. 'We'll have to tell the others that. Now let's see – three barrows; and look, wouldn't it be easier to *shovel* up the onions, instead of picking them up in twos and threes as we said?'

'Now *you're* quite bright!' said Peter. 'I'll go to the tool shed and see what I can find. Hope the gardener's not there. He's a bit gloomy this morning. If the others come, ask them the password and see they've got their badges on.'

Janet began to put the onions into one of the barrows. She had put in about twenty when Colin and George came along.

'Hallo!' said Janet. 'Password, please.'

'It's so long since we had a meeting that we've forgotten it,' said Colin. 'Anyway, we'll hear it when the others come. It's only when we enter the shed that we have to say it. Do *you* know it, Janet?'

'Yes,' said Janet. 'But I had to look it up in my diary. I'd better not tell you it, in case Peter is cross. Come on – help me with the onions. Oh, wait a minute. Have you got your badges on? Good! Peter told me to look and see.'

'This sounds quite like old times,' said Colin. 'We oughtn't to have gone so long without a meeting.' He began to scoop up onions in his hands.

'Here are Pam and Barbara,' said Janet, hearing footsteps. 'Hallo, you two! Password, please!'

Colin and George pricked up their ears at once. Aha – now they would know it!

'Wee Willie Winkie,' said the two girls together, and Janet nodded. 'That's right,' she said. 'Er – password, boys?'

Colin and George repeated it solemnly, and Pam giggled. 'You'd forgotten it,' she said. 'I say – what a lot of onions.'

Peter came back at that moment with Scamper at his heels. He carried one big spade and two small ones.

'Password!' said George, pointing at him. 'And it's *not* Jack the Giant-Killer!'

'Quite right. It's Wee Willie Winkie!' said Peter, with a grin. 'Isn't it, Scamper?'

'Wuff,' said Scamper, pleased to see so many people.

'Let's see — Jack's not come yet,' said Peter. 'Ah — here he is. Has he got his badge on? He said it had gone to the cleaner's on his blazer, and hadn't come back. I told him he'd have to ask his mother to make him another.'

'Hallo, hallo!' said Jack, coming up at a run. 'Am I last? Sorry — but I quite forgot that I'd lost my badge. I went to ask Mother to make one and . . .'

'But that looks like your *old* one on your coat,' said Janet. 'A bit scruffy!'

'It *is* my old one,' said Jack. 'And what's more Susie found it for me! She said that when cleaners find brooches or badges or anything like that on clothes sent to be cleaned, they pop them into an envelope and put them in a pocket. And Susie looked in the breast pocket of my blazer, and there was my badge, inside a little envelope. I'd have been awfully late if she hadn't found it.'

'Well! Fancy *Susie* doing you a good turn!' said George, astonished. 'Good for *her*! We're all here now — let's buck up and move all these onions and get on with the meeting.'

It didn't take long for the seven of them to shovel up the onions into three barrows and wheel them away to the summer-house. Soon they were all neatly piled there and Peter and Jack pulled the old tarpaulin over them to keep them dry.

'Now we'll go back to the shed and hold our meeting,' said Peter. 'We'll get a few boxes to sit on, and after the meeting we'll clear up the shed and make it neat and tidy again.'

Back they all went to the shed. Peter was surprised to

see that the door was now shut, and even more surprised to find Scamper there, growling at it! What *was* the matter with him?

Peter tried to open the door. It was locked from inside! A familiar voice came from the shed, with an aggravating little giggle at the end of it.

'Password, please!'

'*Susie!*' yelled everyone, and Peter shook the door angrily.

'Susie, how dare you? This is *our* meeting-place. Open the door at once.'

'In a minute. I just wanted to sit here and think what a horrible shed this is,' said Susie. 'Pooh! It smells! Now, when I have *my* club, I shan't meet in an onion shed, I shall meet in a . . .'

'Susie! *Will* you open the door?' yelled Peter, banging on it furiously.

'On one condition,' said Susie. 'And that is that you let me walk out without speaking to me or touching me. Otherwise I shall sit here all morning and hold a Secret Seven meeting by myself.'

Peter knew when he was beaten. 'All right, you fathead. Come on out. We want to hold our meeting before the morning's gone. But we'll pay you out for this!'

The door opened and Susie sauntered out, grinning all over her cheeky face. Nobody said a word, though everyone longed to shout at her. She disappeared up the garden path, Scamper giving a few small, rather astonished barks.

'Good riddance to bad rubbish!' said Pam. 'Come on – do let's begin our meeting. My word – I'm glad Susie's not in the Secret Seven. *What* a nuisance she'd be!'

Three

Plenty of plans

THE Seven trooped into the shed and looked round. 'Better get a few boxes, as you said, Peter,' said Janet. 'Pam, you come with me – I know where there are some. You boys sweep out the shed a bit. It's messy with onion skins.'

Before long all the Seven, with Scamper thumping his tail happily on the ground, were seated on boxes round the shed. They felt quite tired after all their shovelling and wheeling of barrows!

'Now, we've met to discuss plans for Bonfire Night,' said Peter, in a business-like way. 'It's still some time ahead, but it takes a good while to save up money for fireworks. Also we'll have to discuss a guy.'

'I vote we make a guy *exactly* like Susie,' said Pam. 'Awful girl!'

'No. Susie would simply *love* that,' said Jack, at once. 'She'd go round boasting about it. I vote we make a nice *big* guy –one that would look fine on top of a bonfire.'

'Oh yes – and let's have a *smashing* bonfire!' said Barbara. 'The biggest we've ever made. We made a pretty big one last year, but I'd like a most enormous one. I love to see the flames blaze high!'

'Right. We'll have a great big bonfire – and a guy to match,' said Peter. 'That means we'll have to begin collecting stuff for it at once. It takes ages to build a big pile of burnable stuff.'

'Where shall we have it?' asked Colin.

'In my garden,' said Barbara. 'Then the next door kids could see it.'

'No. It's too far for us all to bring wood there,' said Peter. 'Actually I think it would be a good idea to have it in the big field just at the bottom of our garden here – for one thing there's a lot of dead wood in the hedges and in the little wood nearby, and it wouldn't be very far to carry it.'

'Yes. That's a good idea,' said Jack. 'We could have a simply enormous one out there in the field. We could meet in the wood, and collect dead twigs and branches together – that would be more fun that getting it on our own and dragging it here.'

'Right. That's settled then,' said Peter 'We're getting on. Now about saving up for fireworks.'

'We'll all bring what we can, as we usually do,' said Barbara. 'I've got a bit of money in my savings box already that I can bring. Who shall be treasurer?'

'Better vote for one,' said Peter. He took out his notebook and tore a page from it. He then tore the page into seven neat strips, and handed a strip to each person. 'Everyone got a pencil?' he said. 'You haven't, Pam – well take mine for a minute. Now – write down the person you think would be a good treasurer – someone to hold the money for us, and keep it safe, and count it each time we bring any. They'll have to keep the figures in a book, so that we know what we've got, and who brought it. Ready? Write the name down then of the one you want. If must be someone good at figures, of course. We don't want a muddle made of our money.'

They all sucked or chewed their pencils and frowned. A good treasurer? One who could manage figures well? One who wouldn't make a muddle?

They each scribbled a name on their piece of paper, folded it and handed it in to Peter. He unfolded each one – and then grinned.

'Hm – well!' he said. 'You all seem to think *I'm* the one – six votes for me! Thanks awfully.'

'But there are seven of us!' said Pam, surprised. 'Who didn't vote for you?'

'*I* didn't vote for myself, silly!' said Peter. 'Actually I voted for Jack. Well, that's settled. We'll meet here in the shed each Saturday at ten o'clock – unless we make different plans. Bring any firework money you have then. And when it's all written down in our fireworks book, we'll go off into the field and the wood and collect stuff for the bonfire.'

'Good,' said George, pleased. 'It's fun to be doing something again. We oughtn't to let so much time go by without a meeting.'

'What about a guy?' asked Colin. 'Who's going to see about him?'

'I think the three girls had better make a big, stuffed body,' said Peter. 'They are more likely to get stuff for the guy than we are. And they can sew better than we can.'

'Gracious – you can't sew at *all*!' said Janet. 'I've just thought of something. Mother said that old eiderdown off your bed was no good now – it's got the moth in. We could use that for the body – all nicely squashed up.'

'Oh *yes*,' said Barbara. 'That's a very good idea. And I believe we've got a dirty old rug somewhere in the loft at home too – that would help to make a good fat body!'

'Well, you girls have got some good ideas,' said Peter. 'We'll decide about clothes at another meeting. We'd better see the size of the guy's body before we try to fit him out with clothes.'

'Don't make him *too* enormous,' said Jack. 'Else we shan't be able to get old clothes to fit him!'

'Well – I think it's time we brought this very interesting meeting to an end,' said Peter. 'What about sweeping out this shed, and getting that old table we had, and putting up a shelf again?'

'Yes. We'll do that,' said Colin, getting up. 'Oh sorry, Scamper – did I tread on your tail? Hallo – who's this coming? If it's Susie, let's all chase her up the path!'

But it wasn't Susie. It was Peter's mother, carrying a tray of lemonade and biscuits.

'I don't know the password!' she said. 'But please let me in. If I say "Lemonade and biscuits!" will that do?'

'Oh Mother – you *are* a brick!' said Peter, in delight. He opened the door. 'Come in – we're all here – and we've had a *marvellous* meeting, and made all kinds of plans!'

'Well, it's nice to see the Secret Seven together again,' said his mother, setting down the tray on a box. 'There now – there are a few dog biscuits for Scamper, because I know he doesn't like being left out.'

'Wuff-wuff!' said Scamper, gratefully, and licked her hand.

Everyone settled down to eat and drink. They felt very happy. They had made plans – good ones too – and they could all work together once more, and meet each week – perhaps oftener.

'Well – here's to Bonfire Night!' said Peter, lifting up his glass. 'And a Jolly Big Guy!'

Four

Saturday morning

THE next Saturday morning all the Seven met again.
'Wee Willie Winkie!' said everyone, and passed quickly
into the shed. Peter shot a sharp look at each of them –
yes, they all had on their badges – good!

The shed looked very neat and tidy now, swept out,
and with sand sprinkled all over the floor by Peter, except
where an old rug lay, given by Pam's mother. Two shelves
were up, and on them stood some plastic cups and a plate
or two. There was also a tin of toffees, and a second tin in
which were home-made biscuits made by Peter's
mother.

Scamper went to sit under the biscuit shelf, looking up
longingly, giving little whines every now and again.

'No, Scamper – it's not biscuit-time yet,' said Peter.
'Don't take any notice of him, anyone. He's had a good
breakfast already. Scamper, be quiet.'

'I've got a report to make on the guy,' said Pam, im-
portantly. 'He's coming along nicely.'

'Fine,' said Peter. 'Tell us about him.'

'Well, we took Barbara's old rug,' said Pam, 'and
Janet's old eiderdown – goodness, it *was* moth-eaten! It's
a good thing it's going to be burnt.'

'And we did a bit of rolling up and shaping,' said Janet,
'and really, it's not a bad body at all. Would you like to see
it? It's just behind the shed, covered over with an old
rubber sheet.'

'You shouldn't leave it there,' said Jack. 'Susie might
get it.'

Janet went to fetch the guy's body. It certainly was

quite fat, and the girls had really managed to shape it very well. It had a round head, a plump body, with a rope tied round it for a waist, and plump arms and legs.

'We haven't made the feet and hands yet!' said Janet. 'It's not bad, is it?'

Scamper was amazed to see such a curious-looking creature. He barked frantically, and seemed quite scared of it. The children laughed at him.

'Wait till it's all dressed up, Scamper,' said Janet. 'You'll bark all right then!'

'If any of us have old clothes that will fit this big fellow, please bring them to our next meeting,' said Peter. 'Or give them to Janet before that, if you can.'

'The guy had better be kept in here, hadn't it?' said Jack. 'If Susie comes snooping round, she *might* find it outside – and she's still thinking of making a club of her own, you know. If she does, they're sure to make a raid on the shed!'

'All right, we'll leave it here – right at the back, in its rubber sheet,' said Janet. 'I'm glad you all approve of it. Please don't forget to look out some nice big clothes – and a big hat or cap. We shall put a mask on him, and he'll look really fine.'

'Now about money,' said Peter. 'Anyone brought any?'

To everyone's delight, the money poured in! Five pence from Pam, ten pence from Barbara, eight pence from Colin, nine pence from George, three pence from Jack, and twenty pence between Peter and Janet.

'Fifty-five pence already,' said Peter, writing down names and money quickly, and adding it up. 'Pretty good.'

'Sorry about my three pence,' said Jack. 'But my Gran

had a birthday this week, and I spent most of my money on a present. I'll bring more next week. Dad has promised me fifteen pence if I'll clean up the garage for him. I'll bring that.'

'That's all right,' said Peter. 'We've made a jolly good start. Now, what about a biscuit or two, and then we'll set off to look for dead wood for our bonfire.'

'Wuff!' said Scamper, at once, thumping his tail on the ground.

Everyone laughed.

'I don't know whether you deserve a biscuit, Scamper,' said Peter. 'You haven't brought in any money – you didn't help with the guy, and . . .'

'Wuff-wuff-wuff!' said Scamper, running over to Peter and putting a paw on his knee.

'He says, can he have a biscuit if he goes and picks up dead wood with us,' said Peter, solemnly. 'Shall we let him?'

'Yes!' shouted everyone, and Scamper received the very first biscuit out of the tin. Everyone took one, and then, locking the shed behind them, they set off, munching their own biscuits, to the field behind Peter's garden.

'Let's choose a place for the bonfire,' said Peter. 'Not too near the hedge, in case it gets burnt.'

'Just here then,' said Jack, walking to a nice flat patch. 'It's well away from the hedge, and we can all dance round it with plenty of room to spare, and let off fireworks.'

Everyone agreed, and Peter nodded. 'Another thing settled,' he said. 'Hallo, look – there's Dad's hedger-and-ditcher man. He might let us have all the trimmings to burn!'

An old fellow was standing a little way up the hedge, slashing at it with a sharp-edged tool. He was cutting away the untidy new growth made that year, and was shaping the hedge skilfully. The children went to him and watched him, admiring the way he cut and trimmed.

'Good morning, Burton,' said Peter. 'You're making a jolly good job of that. Do you like hedging and ditching? You've cleared out the ditch well.'

'I likes any job that takes me outdoors,' said the old fellow. 'Sun and wind and rain, that's what I likes.'

'Could we have the hedge trimmings, do you think?' asked Peter. 'For a bonfire on Guy Fawkes Night?'

'You be welcome to them,' said Burton. 'I'll leave this little lot here for you. Take them any time.'

'Oh good,' said Peter. 'We'll do that. Come along, all of you. We'll be off to the wood now, and hope we'll find stacks of dead wood. We're going to have a jolly busy morning!'

And across the field they ran to the wood, Scamper barking joyfully. What were the Secret Seven up to now? Scamper would help them, whatever it was!

Five

A nasty-looking lot

THE Seven shuffled through the dead leaves in the wood. Except for the evergreen trees, the wood seemed very bare, and full of light. Peter kicked at a fallen branch.

'Here's a nice bit of wood for our fire! Let's make it the beginning of our collection, and bring whatever we find to this spot here under this big tree. Jack and I have brought plenty of rope. We can tie the whole lot up here when we've collected it, and drag it home.'

'Good idea,' said Colin. 'Let's separate then and hunt in different directions.'

The wood was full of dead twigs and fallen branches. There had been a great gale three weeks before, and a good deal of dead or rotten wood had been blown down. The children were delighted to see so much. Soon they each had quite big bundles.

'I'm going to put my lot down where we planned we would,' said Pam. 'I keep dropping bits now. I've got so much.'

'I'll do the same,' said Janet. 'My word, look at Jack over there. He's dragging along half a tree! That's a jolly good find!'

It was fun in the wood, shuffling through the dead leaves, hunting for firewood. One by one the Seven dragged their finds through the trees to the place they had arranged, under the big tree. Soon quite a good pile was there – big twigs, little twigs, small branches, big ones –

and good gracious, here came Peter, Jack and Colin drag-ging a most enormous branch!

'We'll have to chop this one up smaller,' panted Peter. 'I say – we *are* getting on, aren't we?'

'Let's go to the hedger's old hut and sit down for a bit,' said Jack. 'I'm really quite puffed. I've got two packets of sweets to share out. Let's go and sit down and eat them.'

'Good idea,' said Peter, and the Seven set off to Burton's little hut, where he often had his dinner on a rainy day. It was just inside the wood, overgrown with brambles and ivy, and in the summer-time it was so green with the leaves that it could hardly be seen.

'I haven't been here before,' said Pam, as they came near to the hut. 'It must be nice to have a little hut all your own like this. I suppose Burton won't mind us sitting in it, will he?'

'Oh no. Janet and I have often been inside,' said Peter.

Scamper suddenly began to bark as they came near the hut. Peter looked at him in surprise. 'What's the matter, old thing? There's nobody about – not even a rabbit!'

The spaniel stood quite still, his silky nose pointing towards the shed. 'Wuff-wuff-WUFF!' he barked.

'Can't be anyone here,' said Peter. 'Go and look, Scamper. You're just making a fuss.'

Scamper went slowly and stiffly over towards the shed, growling. Everyone watched, puzzled. He went right to the shed door, and then let off a loud volley of barks. An angry voice came from the shed.

'Clear off!' Then a stone came flying out, narrowly missing the surprised Scamper.

Peter raced up to the shed at once, and stood angrily at

the door, glaring at three men inside. 'What do you mean
by throwing stones at my dog? You nearly hit him. You
might have lamed him.'

There came the sound of scornful laughter and then a
stone came spinning out of the shed door and caught
Peter on the ankle.

Scamper gave a fierce growl and darted forward. Peter
just caught him in time before he went into the shed.

'You'd better get out of this shed,' cried the boy,
angrily. 'It doesn't belong to you. It's Burton's hut. I'll
fetch him over here to you if you don't clear out.'

He stood glaring at the three laughing men, and one of
them sent another stone skimming through the door. It
just missed Scamper. 'I'll go and get Burton,' shouted
Peter, and turned to go. He ran back to the others, who
were all standing together, amazed.

'I'm going to get Burton,' panted Peter. 'Watch and see
if the men go.'

He shot off to find Burton, but before he had time to
come back, the three men came out of the shed, stood at
the doorway a few seconds, and stared at the watching
children. One of them shook his fist. The boys pushed the
three girls behind them, as the men walked towards them.
But they turned off between the trees, and disappeared,
talking in low voices.

'What a nasty-looking lot,' said Janet, relieved to see
them go. 'I wonder what they were up to in that shed?'

'Planning some kind of mischief, I should think,' said
Colin. 'It would be a jolly good meeting-place for three
rogues.'

'I've got a notebook,' said Jack. 'I'm going to jot down
what the men are like – just in *case* it might be useful.'

'But how could it be?' said Pam.

'You never know,' said Jack. 'Hallo, here's Peter. Didn't you get Burton?'

'No – he's gone off somewhere,' panted Peter. 'Those men gone?'

'Yes,' said Colin. 'And Jack's just going to jot down some notes about them. We think they're probably plotting some kind of mischief. Let's see – one man was short and dark, and had a crooked nose . . .'

'Yes,' said Jack, writing. 'And one was big and fat, and had a moustache. No hat. Gingery hair.'

'And the third one was thin, and limped,' said Pam. 'His ears stuck out too. I noticed them.'

Jack finished scribbling and put his notebook away.

'Now let's take all our stuff back,' he said. 'Where are the ropes, Peter? Let's have the sweets in our own shed – I don't fancy Burton's shed after those scruffy-looking men have been there!'

Six

The bonfire is begun

PETER had three lengths of rope tied round his waist, and he now untied them and gave one each to Jack and George.

'Make a big bundle of wood and tie it with the rope,' he said. 'Come on, girls – you help me with my bundle!'

They were soon busy tying up the collected wood into enormous bundles. Then they put the ropes over their shoulders, and set off through the trees, pulling the bundles across the field to the place planned for their bonfire.

'This is fun,' said Janet, as she and Peter dragged one great bundle over the field. 'Oh Pam – look, some of our bits have dropped out. You walk behind and pick them up for us.'

In about half an hour's time all the twigs and rotten branches were piled up well. The Seven stood back and looked at the heap proudly, Scamper wagging his tail as though he too had helped with the bundles! But all he had done was to carry one long twig back in his mouth, banging it against Peter's legs!

'There!' said Peter. 'That's a jolly good beginning, I must say. I tell you what, if anyone has half an hour to spare, I think they should pop along and collect a few more bits and pieces, Janet and I might be able to in our dinner-hour next week.'

'And I could race along from afternoon school perhaps, on my bike, at four o'clock sometime,' said George. 'It would still be light enough to hunt about.'

'Good,' said Peter. 'Every little helps, as my Dad says when he wants us to go weeding, and hopes we'll do half the garden!'

'Let's go and sit down and have Jack's sweets,' said Pam. 'I feel quite tired out.'

They left the pile of wood and went to sit in their own shed. Peter unlocked the door and they went in.

'I'm keeping the door locked because I've got our firework money in that box on the shelf,' he said. 'And also because of the guy. Susie just *might* come along and do something silly to it.'

'She wouldn't touch the money, though, you know that jolly well,' said Jack at once.

Peter nodded. 'Yes. I know that, of course. Come on – hand out the sweets, Jack. It's nearly dinner-time, but I bet they won't spoil our appetites. Not mine anyway, because we're having steak and kidney pudding, and *nothing* would put me off that.'

'*Why* did you have to mention steak and kidney?' groaned George. 'You've made me feel so hungry that I could eat all Jack's sweets at one go.'

Jack hastily stuffed the sweets back into his pocket. His hand touched his notebook, and he remembered that he had written the three men's descriptions in it. He drew it out, and read them out loud.

'It will be funny if we meet them again,' he said. 'We shall know where they're going – probably to Burton's hut in the woods.'

'We shan't meet them again – not in Burton's hut or anywhere else,' said Colin. 'They were just tramps, wandering over the country. They sat down for a rest in the hut, I expect.'

'Oh well – you never know,' said Jack, rather damped,

and put his notebook back into his pocket. 'When's our next meeting, Peter?'

'Can you manage Thursday afternoon, after school?' said Peter. 'Not for finding wood, but just for seeing what guy clothes we get and if anyone has some more money. Then we shan't have to spend so much time on those things next Saturday morning; we can get straight on with collecting wood for the bonfire.'

'Right,' said Colin, and George and Jack nodded too.

'Pam and I may not be able to come,' said Barbara. 'We may have an extra dancing lesson then. We're in a concert soon, you know.'

'Well, come if you can,' said Peter. 'Same password – and badges, of course. There's our dinner-bell. We must go. See you on Monday, chaps!'

They all departed, and Peter and Janet and Scamper went up the path to their house.

'Wash your hands!' called their mother. 'My goodness me, you *are* dirty!'

'We've been collecting wood for our bonfire,' called back Janet. 'We won't be a minute.'

They told their mother all about their morning as they ate their steak and kidney pudding very hungrily indeed. When they came to the piece about the three men in the hut, their mother looked up sharply.

'Now listen – you are not to go into the wood unless there are at least three or four of you – certainly not alone. I don't like the sound of those men. There are some very bad men about in these days.'

'But Mother, they were only tramps,' said Peter. 'And anyway, Scamper was with us.'

'Well, if you go into the wood you are to take Scamper

with you,' said Mother. 'And you are not to let any of the girls wander about without you boys. Now that's an *order*. Do you understand, or shall I get Daddy to say so?'

'No – of course not. We'll do exactly what you say,' said Peter, surprised. 'Mother, you should just *see* our bonfire pile of wood – it's awfully big already.'

'I shall have to come and watch it when you set it alight,' said his mother. 'And see the fireworks too. By the way, Janet, if you want to earn firework money, you can do a little job for me.'

'Oh good. What, Mother?' asked Janet.

'You can turn out the linen cupboard and put back everything tidily for me,' said his mother. 'That will be a five pence job if you do it well.'

'Right, I'd love to,' said Janet. 'I like arranging things. I'll do it this very evening. Our next meeting is on Thursday, you know.'

But their next meeting came before Thursday after all. Something very exciting happened – and it was Colin who called the meeting, not Peter!

Seven

Colin has some news

On Monday evening, when Peter and Janet were sitting quietly doing their homework, the telephone rang. Mother went to answer it.

She called to Peter. 'It's for you, Peter. Colin wants to speak to you. He sounds very excited.'

Peter shot to the telephone at once, and Janet went too. What had happened? Colin had walked part of the way home from school with Peter that afternoon, and hadn't seemed in the least excited about anything.

'Hallo? Peter here,' said Peter, and at once heard Colin's excited voice. 'Peter, can I come and see you *at once*? Something's happened. I want to call a meeting of the Secret Seven as soon as possible – tomorrow after school perhaps. Can I come right along now? I'll only be a minute or two on my bike.'

'Goodness – what's the matter?' said Peter, astonished. 'A meeting? Whatever about?'

'Can't tell you now. People might hear,' said Colin. This sounded very mysterious indeed.

'Well, come along at once,' said Peter. 'Better come to the shed. We'll be alone there. See you soon.'

He put down the receiver, and stared at Janet, who was just beside him.

'What is it?' she said, excited.

'Don't know,' said Peter. 'He's coming in a few minutes – to the shed. He wants to call a meeting of the Secret Seven tomorrow. Whatever *can* be the matter?'

'I'm coming down to the shed too,' said Janet.

'No, you're not,' said Peter. 'All right, all right – don't look so fierce. I'll let you come, but remember, not a word to anyone unless I say so.'

'As if I *would* say anything!' said Janet, scornfully. 'Mother! Mother, where are you? Peter and I are going to slip down to our shed for a minute. Colin wants to see us about something important.'

'Aha! Secret Seven business, I suppose,' said her mother. 'All right, but put coats on, please. It will be cold down there tonight.'

They put on their coats and slipped down to the shed, with Scamper trotting happily at their heels. Peter un-locked the door, and lighted a little oil-lamp his mother had given him for the shed. He set it carefully on a box.

The two waited patiently for Colin, trying in vain to think what could have excited him so. It must be some-thing very important if he wanted to call a meeting! Any member had the right to do this, though as a rule it was only Peter who did so.

Jingle-jingle! That was a bicycle bell. *Click* – that was the front gate. Then came the sound of footsteps as Colin hurried down the path to the shed, wheeling his bicycle.

He rapped at the door. 'Wee Willie Winkie,' he said, in a low voice, and Peter opened the door at once.

'What's all the excitement about?' Peter asked. 'Sit down and tell us.'

'I'll begin at the beginning,' said Colin, whose face was red with cycling fast and with excitement. 'You know where my granny lives, don't you? Not far from my house, but round the corner?'

'Yes,' said Peter and Janet together.

'Well, she's away,' said Colin, 'but she's coming back

tomorrow, so my mother asked me if I'd take some new-laid eggs to Granny's house – we keep hens, you know – and give them to Greta, her Austrian maid, so that Granny could have some poached eggs when she gets back. It's her favourite meal.'

He stopped and rubbed his hot face with his hanky.

'Go on,' said Peter. 'Do come to the point.'

'I *am*,' said Colin. 'Well, I took the eggs and ran up the road and round the corner. There was a light in the hall as usual – but I didn't knock at the front door, because I always go in the back way. It saves Greta coming to the door. Well, I slipped round the back way, and got to the kitchen door. It was shut, but not locked.'

'Wuff!' said Scamper, suddenly, and made them all jump.

'It's all right – he only saw a mouse run over the floor,' said Janet. 'Do go on.'

'I went inside,' said Colin. 'Greta wasn't in the kitchen, so I went through to the sitting-room. There was a light there, and I wondered if Granny had got back a day early, I pushed open the door – and my word *what* a mess I saw! Phew!'

'What kind of a mess?' asked Peter, thrilled.

'Everything upside down – drawers pulled out and emptied on the floor. The cupboard broken open. And then I saw Granny's safe – that was broken open too! She had it behind a big mirror – I didn't know that before. Someone had taken down the mirror, found the safe and smashed it open. It was empty!'

'*Colin!* How *awful*!' said Janet.

'Where was Greta?' said Peter. 'Surely *she* hadn't done all that!'

'Of *course* not,' said Colin. 'I suddenly heard a wailing

noise, and rushed out into the hall. I traced the noise to the kitchen – and then to the larder, which was locked on the outside. I unlocked the door – and there was poor Greta inside, locked in!'

'What did you do next?' asked Peter, really excited.

'I telephoned the police,' said Colin. 'I felt frightfully important, ringing up the police-station. Two men came round at once – and by that time my mother and father were there too, because I phoned them as well.'

'But why do you want to call a meeting of the Secret Seven about this?' asked Peter. '*We* can't do anything.'

'Well, listen,' said Colin. 'I heard Greta giving details of the robbers to the police – three men – and she described two of them *exactly* as Jack described those men in his notebook – the men we saw. Greta didn't see the third – but I'm *sure* they must have been the men we saw in Burton's hut – and for all we know they were planning the robbery then!'

'Whew!' said Peter. 'Think of that! Yes – we'll certainly call a meeting tomorrow. After afternoon school sharp at quarter past four. My word – what a thrill!'

Eight

Another meeting

TUESDAY seemed a very long day indeed to the Secret Seven. They longed for afternoon school to be over so that they could race off to the meeting-shed, and hear all that Colin had to say. He had actually been called out of school that morning by the police, who wanted to ask him questions!

'I bet he feels jolly important,' said Jack to Peter, as Colin walked out of the schoolroom. 'I'm longing for our meeting, aren't you?'

The meeting time came at last. Everyone was at the shed very punctually indeed, except Jack, who arrived last of all, panting for breath.

'Wee Willie Winkie,' he gasped. 'Sorry to be last, but it was Susie's fault. She wanted to know what was up, and when I wouldn't tell her, she went and hid my bike – and her own too – so I had to run all the way here on my feet.'

'Sit down,' said Peter. 'Colin, begin your story, please.'

Colin told it all over again. He was sorry that it was his granny's house that had been robbed, but he couldn't help feeling very thrilled that he had been the one to discover the robbery, and telephone the police.

'So Greta saw two of the men, but not the third,' said Peter, when Colin had finished. 'Have you brought your notebook, Jack? I rather think we shall find the description of the third robber there!'

Jack fumbled for his notebook, his face alight with excitement. 'To think I wrote down all their descriptions –

just by chance, really, because I happened to have my notebook!' he said. 'Wait a minute – yes, here are my notes. Colin, how did Greta describe the two men *she* saw?'

'She said one was very short and dark,' said Colin, 'and she specially noticed that his nose was crooked, and she said he had bad teeth.'

'Well, that answers exactly to my first description,' said Jack, excited. 'I've got "One man was short and dark, and had a crooked nose". I didn't notice his bad teeth.'

'The crooked nose is enough, really,' said Colin. 'Well, that was one man. Greta said the second man was thin, and had ears that stuck out from his head. She said she thought he was lame, but she wasn't sure about that.'

'Ha – she's right!' said Jack, looking at his notes again. 'Listen. I've got one man down as thin, and noted that he limped – well, that's Greta's second robber, no doubt about that! You say she didn't see the other one?'

'No – she said that the men burst in at the kitchen door, and she saw the first two quite clearly. The third man was behind them, so she couldn't describe him. The first two leapt at her, and she fell to the floor, poor Greta. They turned her on her face, and the third man bound her hands, and then they bundled her into the larder and locked the door. She wasn't really hurt – only scared stiff.'

'She must have been thrilled to see you when you opened the larder!' said Janet.

'She was! I undid her hands, and she put her arms round my neck and hugged me, and said hundreds of things in German, which I couldn't understand at all,' said Colin. 'Then she sat down, plump, on a chair – and *most* unluckily it was where I'd put the bag of eggs.'

Everyone roared with laughter, and then stopped, looking rather guilty.

'We oughtn't to have laughed,' said Janet. 'It's all very serious – but honestly – when I thought of poor Greta sitting down on Colin's eggs, I just couldn't help myself!'

'Well, Greta laughed too, when she found out,' said Colin. 'Actually she laughed and cried at the same time. Gosh, I did have a time – seeing to Greta, and telephoning the police and Mother and Dad – and waiting for the police to arrive – well, honestly, I half thought it must all be a dream!'

'I bet you did,' said Peter. 'Did you tell the police that you thought we'd seen the three men?'

'Yes, I did,' said Colin. 'But I didn't say anything about Jack writing down the descriptions of them, because I thought perhaps he'd like to tell them that himself. I mean – it might be an important clue.'

'Jolly decent of you,' said Jack. 'Shall we go to the police together, straight away now, Colin, with my notebook?'

'Yes, you'd better,' said Peter. 'They'll be interested to know we've got descriptions of the third man. Or rather, that you have, Jack. Good thing you wrote them down – you just *never* know when a thing like that is going to be useful.'

'I think we'll go now,' said Jack, getting up, looking rather important. 'Come on, Colin.'

'Thanks for calling the meeting, Peter,' said Colin. 'Can we have another soon – to tell you what happens at the police-station when Jack and I give them the third man's description?'

'Rather – tomorrow, same time,' said Peter. 'And I'll see if my mother will let us have tea down here in the shed. See you tomorrow then, Jack and Colin.'

They were just getting up when Scamper began to bark loudly and excitedly. Then there came a loud knock at the door, which made them all jump.

'Open in the name of the law,' said a queer, deep voice.

'Gracious – it's the police again,' said Colin, and opened the door.

There was no one there! The Seven stared out into the half-darkness, feeling just a bit scared. Scamper raced out, barking, and stopped by a bush. Peter ran up to it, and shone his torch there. A delighted giggle greeted him.

'*Susie!*' yelled everyone, in a fury.

'Please, Peter, I've brought poor Jack's bicycle for him to ride home on,' said the maddening Susie. 'I thought he'd be pleased.'

'You horrid little snooper!' shouted Jack. But Susie had gone, slipping away in the darkness. How much had she heard? *What* a little wretch she was!

Nine

Susie really is annoying

COLIN and Jack cycled off to the police-station at once, Jack with his precious notebook in his pocket. When they got to the station, they found the sergeant there, a man they liked very much. He had already seen Colin twice – once when the police had gone to his granny's house, in answer to his telephone call, and once when they had called him out of school that morning, to ask him questions.

'Hallo, Colin – you again!' said the sergeant, and smiled. 'Well – got any more burglars to report?'

'No, sir,' said Colin. 'But Jack here has the description of the third man – the one Greta didn't see.'

'Well, I'm blessed!' said the sergeant, and pulled a note-pad in front of him. 'We've got pretty good descriptions of two of the men, but not the third. Greta didn't see him, as you just now said. How do *you* know what he was like? You said you didn't see anyone yourself, at the house.'

'No, sir,' said Colin. 'You see, it's like this. We were out in the woods last Saturday, and we came to a hut, and inside were three men. They were pretty awful to us and we thought they might be up to some mischief. So Jack here wrote down their descriptions. Jack, give your notes to the sergeant.'

Jack handed them over. The sergeant read them quickly. He whistled when he came to 'One was big and fat, and had a moustache. No hat. Gingery hair.' He put the notebook down and looked at Jack.

'Good work, son,' he said. 'Really, kids are pretty smart nowadays! Your description of two of them is excellent – we're pretty certain we know who they are, though we don't know *where* they are. I can't place the third one – the big, fat fellow, with a moustache and gingery hair. What was he dressed in? Did you notice?'

'Well no,' said Jack, trying to remember. 'They were all pretty dirty and scruffy. Nothing outstanding in their clothes, as far as I can remember. Did you notice anything in the way they were dressed, Colin?'

'No. I just think they were in overcoats of some sort,' said Colin, frowning. 'Two of them wore hats or, caps – and I know one hadn't a hat – that was the red-haired fellow, of course. We all noticed his hair, because he had no hat.'

'Well, this is a great help,' said the sergeant, giving Jack back his notebook. 'I expect those thieves are miles away by now, but keep your eyes open, will you – you and the others?'

'We certainly will, sir,' said both boys together. They said goodnight, and left the police-station, both feeling very thrilled at having been able to help.

'We'll tell the others all this at the meeting tomorrow night,' said Jack. 'Golly, I'll have to race home! I've loads of homework to do. Wait till I see that sister of mine – pretending she was the police tonight, and making us open our shed-door to her! Perhaps she won't interfere so much in future though – she's having two friends to stay with her – both girls, whose mother's in hospital. Susie will be so busy looking after them that she won't have time to interfere with the Secret Seven.'

'Good thing!' said Colin, who heartily disliked the aggravating Susie. 'We don't want her poking her nose into this!'

They parted and went their separate ways. Jack went to find Susie as soon as he got home, to tick her off for breaking in on their meeting that night.

'Susie!' he yelled, as soon as he got in. 'Where are you? What do you mean by pretending to ... oh, sorry, I thought you were Susie!'

'No. I'm Doris, who's come to stay,' said the girl he had thought was Susie. 'And this is Hilda, my sister. It's nice of your mother to have us. I hope we shan't be in the way.'

Jack looked at Doris and Hilda, and he didn't much like what he saw. They grinned at him impudently, he thought, and he didn't look forward to having *three* giggling girls talking about him, and nudging each other, and playing jokes on him. One was bad enough!

'Open in the name of the law!' said a voice – Susie's, of course. 'Oh, Jack – did you really think I . . .'

'You behaved abominably,' said Jack. 'Breaking in on our meeting like that. I was ashamed of you.'

'We're going to make a little club ourselves – Hilda, Doris and I,' said Susie. 'It's called the Tiresome Three.'

'I should think it's a very good name,' said Jack. 'So long as you don't make yourselves tiresome to *us*, and keep away when we're meeting.'

'Oh, the grand Secret Seven!' said Susie. She turned to the giggling Hilda and Doris. 'You've no idea how solemn their silly old meetings are,' she said. 'Passwords, badges, nobody else allowed in, oh, they think they're too grand for words. You look out, Jack – the Tiresome Three might come and join you one night!'

'Shall we raid their shed?' said Doris. 'That's what my

brother and his club did to another club – they got a lot of things, they got . . .'

'If you *dare* to interfere with us, *any* of you, I'll – I'll pull your hair off!' cried Jack, exasperated, and marched out of the room, boiling over.

'What a bad-tempered brother you've got, Susie,' he heard Hilda say, and he very nearly turned back to pull her hair. He went to his room and sat down, frowning. Never mind! *Let* them laugh and giggle! The Secret Seven were helping the police, and he couldn't see the Tiresome Three helping *any*one!

'I'll have to warn the Seven that Susie and the others mean to make trouble,' he thought, as he took his home-work from his school bag. 'Thank goodness we've got old Scamper – he always barks when anyone comes near the shed. How *dare* Susie do the things she does!'

Ten

A wonderful guy

PETER asked his mother if he could have the Secret Seven to tea the next day, Wednesday.

'You see, Mother, what with one thing and another, there seems to be a lot to talk about and plan – Bonfire Night, of course, and now this business of Colin's Granny being robbed, and us having seen the three men . . .'

'We'll see to the tea ourselves, Mother, you don't need to do a thing,' said Janet. 'And we won't scamp our homework, we promise you.'

'All right, dears – of course you can have a Secret Seven tea,' said their mother. 'I'll cut the bread and butter, and I'll bake you some biscuits, and you can buy some buns or something at the baker's. I shan't have time to make cakes too. Do you want lemonade or tea?'

'Oh, lemonade – no, orangeade for a change!' said Peter. '*We'll* carry everything down, Mother, and we'll wash up, too. You're always so *decent* about the Secret Seven.'

'Well, if you want to know something – I'm very glad I've got a decent son, who runs a decent club, helped by a very decent sister!' said Mother, laughing.

Everyone was very punctual at the meeting, and their eyes shone when they saw the spread provided for them.

'I'm glad I didn't eat too much dinner today,' said Colin, eyeing the currant bread and butter, and the jam sandwich that Janet had bought, and the big plate of home-made biscuits.

They talked as they munched away at their tea, Scamper gnawing happily at a great big bone. Jack told them about Susie and the Tiresome Three. Peter groaned.

'*Don't* say they're going to play silly tricks on us – really, I'm getting awfully tired of Susie,' he said.

'Well, it doesn't much matter if they raid us while we're *here*,' said Janet. 'The door's locked. And if they come when we're not here, the door will still be locked! Even Susie wouldn't break the window, surely, to get in!'

'How are you getting on with the guy?' asked Jack.

'We'll show you, when we begin the meeting,' said Janet. 'We've got some fine clothes for him! Pam's father was a brick. When he heard about the guy, he rummaged through his old clothes, and sent some.'

'You see, Dad's big and rather fat,' said Pam. 'So his clothes should fit the guy beautifully.'

'And George's father gave George a wonderful cap for the guy,' said Janet. 'Your father must have an awfully big head, George – the cap's enormous.'

'He *has* got a big head,' said George, proudly, 'It needs to be big, he's terribly brainy, you know.'

'And our dad gave us some old gum boots – his field boots, simply colossal,' said Peter. 'They might be too big even for the fat legs of the guy!'

'We'll dress him up after the meeting,' said Janet. 'He's there, waiting at the back – he'll be glad to be dressed. He needs a mask, too.'

'I'll slip up to the shops and get one as soon as I've finished tea,' said Colin. 'I don't like guys without faces – they look horrid. I bet old Scamper won't like the mask, though!'

'I hope you've all remembered to bring a little firework money,' said Peter.

'Yes,' said everyone, and Peter grinned, very pleased. He couldn't help thinking that his club must be about the best in the kingdom! Even their dog always behaved well!

The boys carried back the tea-things when tea was over. Then they settled down to the meeting, and Peter took the firework money from each member. He added up the total. 'Whew! One pound and five pence – pretty good, you know – and there's still some time to go. We mustn't forget we've still got to build our bonfire higher.'

'We can collect more wood on Saturday morning,' said George. 'Now, what about dressing the guy?'

They pulled the fat, shapeless body out from its rubber sheet, and sat it on a box. Scamper growled at it at once. He didn't like it at all.

They began to dress it, laughing. It wasn't at all easy.

'It seems as if the old guy just *won't* help us!' panted Jack, trying to pull a pair of enormous trousers over the guy's plump legs. 'Don't be so *awkward*, guy!'

'It's a good thing Pam's father is such a big man,' said Barbara. 'The guy is larger than we thought! What about some braces?'

'Oh, we don't need those. We can safety-pin the trousers to his body,' said Janet. 'There, the trousers are on at last – they make him more real, somehow.'

'Now the coat,' said Jack, taking up a rather stained old tweed coat, that didn't match the trousers.

'That's the coat my dad used when he was plastering and painting our kitchen,' said Pam. 'My mother said she was glad to see the back of it! Aren't the buttons nice? Half-yellow and half-brown. Too good for the guy, really!'

'Well, it fits him beautifully,' said Peter, laughing as he did up the buttons. 'Feeling warmer now, Mr Guy? Colin, what about you going to buy a mask before the shops shut?'

'Right,' said Colin, and slipped out of the shed door. 'Shan't be long.'

The others began to pull the boots on to the guy's plump legs. It really was a hard job.

'He's an obstinate fellow, this guy,' said Jack. 'Wants to go bare-foot, I suppose! There – that boot's on, thank goodness. Stop growling, Scamper. Anyone would think you didn't like our beautiful guy!'

Scamper's growls suddenly became louder and he ran to the door. 'Susie! The Tiresome Three!' said everyone. But they were wrong.

It was Colin, carrying a mask, and in a great state of excitement. He waved an evening paper at them.

'I say! There's news about the thieves who got into my granny's house. They've caught two of them. It's all printed here. Stop messing about with the guy, and listen.'

'Shut the door,' said Peter, sharply, afraid that Susie might be lurking outside, and Colin banged it at once. He sat down on a box, and opened the paper. 'It's here – in the stop press news – this bit in the corner,' he said. 'I'll read it to you.'

Eleven

One up to the Tiresome Three

'Go on – do read it,' said Janet, impatiently.

'*It is reported this afternoon that two of the thieves who robbed Mrs Strangeway's house on Monday night, have been caught by the police. They had not left the district. The third man ran away and escaped. The police have a full description of him. He is stout, tall and has a moustache and red hair. Unfortunately the stolen articles have not yet been recovered. Anyone having seen a man of the above description is asked to contact the police.*'

'Gosh!' said Peter, as Colin finished reading. 'So they've got two of the men already. What a pity the other fellow escaped.'

'Yes – and took the stuff with him, I suppose,' said Colin gloomily. 'My poor old granny is in an awful state, as you can imagine. She had to go to bed with shock as soon as she got back, and my mother sent for the doctor. If only she could get back the things she prized most – my grandfather's silver cups – the ones he won for all kinds of sport – and the jewellery that's been in her family for years. I wish the police had got the stolen stuff instead of the robbers!'

'Probably the two thieves who were caught will soon confess where they hid it,' said Pam.

'Well, I should think the third man, who wasn't caught, will certainly go and take the things from whatever hiding-place they are in now, and hide them somewhere else!' said Peter. 'Just in case his pals gave away the hiding-place! He could then wait a bit till all the hue and cry had died down, and take them for himself!'

'Yes, I suppose he could,' said Colin, laying down the paper. 'Fancy the men still being in the district. You'd have thought they would have got away as soon as possible.'

'I bet the man who's free will have put a hundred miles between himself and the police by now,' said Jack.

'If he hasn't, he'll find it difficult to move about in the daytime,' said Colin.'You can shave off a moustache, but you can't hide your fatness – or your ginger hair.'

'You *can* hide your hair – dye it, say – or wear a hat, silly,' said Barbara.

'Let's get on with the guy,' said Janet. 'What do you think of him, Colin?'

She and Pam pulled the guy in front of Colin. He looked very queer in his big trousers, carefully safety-pinned in place, his enormous dirty old tweed coat, and large rubber boots. Scamper began to bark angrily again.

'He simply can't bear our guy,' said Pam. 'Did you get a mask, Colin? Oh yes, there it is. Put it on the guy, then we can put the cap on his head.'

Colin carefully fitted the big mask over the front of the guy's head. Everyone roared with laughter. The guy seemed very real now he had a face!

'Isn't it odd – you've chosen a mask with a red moustache!' said Janet. 'Like the robber who got away! Mr Guy Fawkes, are you sure you're not the third robber?'

The guy stared solemnly at her, and Scamper growled again. He really did not like the guy at all.

'Take the mask off and squeeze the head a bit to make the mask fit better,' said George. 'It sticks out over his chest too much.'

They took off the mask, and pummelled the stuffed head till it was a better shape. Then on went the mask again, and Scamper gave another volley of angry barks.

'Now the cap,' said George, and solemnly placed it on the guy's head, screwing it round a bit to give it a jaunty, rakish look. The Seven laughed uproariously. The guy looked really comical with his cap on.

'How do you do, Mr Fawkes?' said George, and shook him by the hand. 'I hope you are feeling well, and looking forward to warming yourself on our bonfire next week.'

'He looks awfully uncomfortable sitting on that box,' said Janet. 'And he's heavy to hold up straight. Can't we get him an old chair, or something, to sit in? He'll last a lot longer on top of the bonfire if he's sitting up.'

'I think there's an old chair, with arms, in the stables,' said Peter. 'Nobody uses it now. Let's go and get it, shall we?'

They all trooped out of the shed, Scamper too, leaving the guy sprawled over his box.

'Back in a minute, Mr Fawkes,' said Colin, politely, and made the others laugh.

They made their way to the stables, and there sure enough, in a corner with other jumble, was the old chair. Its cane seat was almost gone, and part of the back. But it still had its two arms.

'Just the thing,' said Peter, pleased. 'We can easily put a bit of wood over the rotten cane seat, for him to sit on. Give me a hand, Colin.'

They took the old chair back to the shed, Peter shining his torch as they went. When they came in sight of the shed, glowing by the light of its little oil-lamp, they stopped in a hurry!

Peter's torch had picked up something standing against the shed, near the open door. Whatever – whoever – was it?

'It's – it's our *guy*!' cried Janet in fright. 'Look – he's walked out of the shed – he's standing there! Peter! Look at him!'

Yes, there was the guy, sure enough, leaning against the shed, quite still, his mask looking exactly like a face. And then – and then came the sound of suppressed giggles from somewhere nearby!

'*Susie!*' yelled Jack, in fury. 'You've taken our guy and stood him outside. Wait till I get you three – how *dare* you!'

There came the sound of more giggles, and then scampering feet. The Tiresome Three, having made their first raid, were gone!

'They've hung him on a nail, look,' said Peter, angrily seeing that the guy's neck was neatly impaled on an old nail at just about the right height. 'Golly – didn't he look real, leaning there against the shed? What on earth possessed us to go off and leave the door open? We must have been mad!'

'Wait till I get home,' said Jack, grimly. 'I'll tick those girls off properly. Here – let's take the guy into the shed again. Come along, Mr Fawkes. Sorry you've had such a silly trick played on you, poor old fellow!'

Twelve

Jack can be tiresome too!

THE Secret Seven were really very angry to think that the Tiresome Three had actually dared to go into their meeting-shed, and take out the guy.

'What idiots we were to leave the shed open, even for those few minutes!' groaned Peter. 'But Scamper didn't bark or growl as he usually does when there's anyone hiding near.'

'I expect they arrived at the very minute we went off to get the chair,' said Colin. 'Just a bit of sheer luck for them, that's all. For goodness sake lock the door each time you leave the shed, Peter. They'll steal the whole guy next, and burn him on their own bonfire. Are they going to have a bonfire, Jack?'

'Don't ask *me*,' said Jack. 'As if they'd tell me anything! Those two girls, Doris and Hilda, are even worse than Susie, it seems to me! Giggle, giggle, giggle, all the time. I expect they *will* have fireworks and a bonfire – I don't know about a guy.'

They sat the guy down in the chair, having first put a sheet of wood under him to stop him sinking down through the broken cane seat. He sat there, his arms on the arms of the chair, looking as if he wanted to smoke a pipe or read a newspaper!

'He's not a bad guy at all,' said Barbara. 'I've never seen such a nice *plump* one before. We could perhaps get him an old pipe – we could stick it into his mouth for him.'

'I say – it's getting pretty late,' said George, looking at his watch. 'I've got homework to do. I must go. That was a jolly good meeting, even if it had an annoying ending. Don't forget to thank your mother for us, Peter. Jolly fine tea!'

The meeting broke up, for not only George had home-work to do. Soon the shed was in darkness, the door se-curely locked, and the key in Peter's pocket. The guy sat there in his chair alone.

Jack cycled back home, fuming with rage. Susie really was behaving badly. What a sister to have! He went to put his bicycle away, and suddenly spotted a faint light in the summer-house down the garden.

'Hallo – who's there?' he thought, and crept down to see. He heard low voices, and recognized them at once.

'Susie – and the others! A meeting of the Tiresome Three, I suppose!' thought Jack, grimly. 'All right – *I'll* do a little snooping this time!'

He stood close to the windows of the summer-house, thinking that it was a remarkably cold spot to choose for a meeting-place. He grinned to himself. What a fine re-venge for Susie's surprise that night!

He heard Susie's voice. 'We can't let the Seven crow over us with a guy like that – and firework money for tons of fireworks – and the biggest bonfire in the district!' she said. 'I wouldn't mind if they'd let us *share* in the fireworks and *see* the bonfire, and help to burn the guy – but they're jolly mean, all of them, and they just won't share a thing.'

'Well, we'll raid them again,' said a voice – it sounded like Hilda's. 'What about their bonfire? Where is it? Can't we raid that?'

'I don't know where it is,' said Susie. 'I can find out,

though. I'll ask Jack quite nicely – and I bet he'll tell me!'

There were a few giggles, and something that Jack couldn't catch. He began to boil with fury. Raid the Secret Seven's *bonfire*! What a nerve!

'It's a pity we've so little money for fireworks,' said Doris. 'They're so frightfully expensive – and it's no fun unless you have a lot. And we haven't a guy, either.'

'It's not much good having a guy unless you've got a bonfire to burn him on,' said Susie. 'Didn't their guy have marvellous clothes? I wish we could get hold of some like that!'

Then came more talk that Jack couldn't hear. The Tiresome Three must have put their heads close together, and were making plans. *What* plans? Jack had great forebodings. What were these awful girls going to do next? He *certainly* wouldn't tell them where the bonfire was! Well, he might *hint* – but it would be a hint that would send them quite in the wrong direction!

Jack began to smile. Yes – he could send the Tiresome Three on a long, long walk – with no bonfire at the end of it! It would serve them right.

Then he thought he would give the girls a fright to pay them out for their night's mischief. He opened his mouth and gave a weird and wonderful groan that startled even himself.

'Oooo-ah-oooo-ee-AHHHH!'

There was a sudden silence in the summer-house. Then he heard Susie's scared voice. 'Gracious! Whatever was that?'

Jack groaned again, ending with a most blood-curdling yowl. With three terrified shrieks the Tiresome Three stumbled out of the summer-house and fled up the garden at top speed. Jack went into the summer-house and collapsed on the seat, holding his sides with laughter.

'Oh my! I really didn't know I could groan like that!' he said. 'Well – I'll saunter into the house now, and pretend I've just come from the Secret Seven meeting.'

So in he strolled, hands in his pockets, humming a tune. The girls turned to him at once, still looking scared.

'Jack! Did you hear a perfectly frightful noise as you came in through the garden?' asked Susie.

'What do you mean? The cat mewing?' said Jack. 'Don't say you're scared of *him*! Or do you mean the old brown owl? You girls! If you heard a mouse squeak you'd skitter off in fright! And by the way, I suppose you think that was funny, taking our guy out of the shed like that? Well, it wasn't. It was just plain mean.'

'Well, aren't *you* mean?' demanded Susie at once. 'You won't share your guy and we haven't one. You won't share your fireworks – and we've none! And I bet you won't even tell us where your bonfire will be – you won't even let us *see* that!'

'Where *is* the bonfire?' said Hilda, looking very innocent. 'Fancy not even telling us that!'

'Oh, I'll tell you where you'll find a bonfire we've built,' said Jack. 'You know Haylings Field, that runs up that very steep hill? Well, you'll find a bonfire there, all ready to light. Now don't you be mean and light it! I don't trust you three giggling fatheads an inch!'

He strolled out of the room, and the Tiresome Three grinned at one another.

'Easy, wasn't it?' said Susie. 'We'll go there tomorrow! *And* we'll pull their bonfire to bits!'

Thirteen

Face at the window

JACK cycled round to Peter's early the next morning to tell him the joke he meant to play on the Tiresome Three. Peter grinned.

'Jolly good idea! I'll cycle up Haylings Hill with you now, and we'll take a few miserable twigs – and a note to put under them! When will the girls go up, do you think?'

'After afternoon school, I imagine,' said Jack. 'Only Susie has a bike, so they'll have to climb all the way up on foot – and you know how steep it is.'

'I'll write a note now,' said Peter, getting out his notebook and pencil. He scribbled something and signed it, then passed it across to Jack.

'YOU CAN HAVE THE WHOLE OF THIS BONFIRE IF YOU LIKE. HOPE YOU EN-JOYED YOUR CLIMB. A GOOD LAUGH FROM — THE SECRET SEVEN.'

Jack chuckled. 'Jolly good. That will make them wild – they'll have all that long climb for nothing! All the same, we'll have to keep an eye on our *real* bonfire, Peter. I wouldn't be in the least surprised if they didn't come and look for it and kick it about, when they find they've been tricked into going up to the top of Haylings Hill.'

'Yes. We'll certainly keep an eye on it. One or other of us had better keep guard there, I suppose,' said Peter. 'What's to-day – Thursday. We'll all meet this afternoon, I think, and we'll take what money anyone brings, and arrange for two of us to go and buy fireworks on Saturday. Better not leave it too late or the best ones will be gone.

Let's see, Bonfire Night is on Sunday – that means we'll have to hold it on Monday.'

'Why not Saturday?' asked Jack.

'Colin said he might not be able to come,' said Peter. 'He asked me *not* to make it Saturday. I'd better get my bike and ride up Haylings Hill with you straight away, or we'll be late for school. Gather a few sticks and twigs while I get it.'

Soon the two boys were cycling off at top speed. In their bicycle baskets was a collection of small twigs. They grinned when they looked at them.

Haylings Hill was very steep indeed. They had to get off their bicycles near the top and push them. At last they were at the summit, and hurriedly arranged a criss-cross of twigs as if for a small fire. Peter stuffed the note under the twigs, so that a corner of it showed.

'There! I hope the Tiresome Three will enjoy their climb!' he said. 'Come on – it's getting late. Thank goodness it's all downhill now!'

The Secret Seven met again in their shed that day at a quarter past five, when everyone had had tea. Scamper was delighted to see them, and leapt round in delight. He couldn't imagine why the Seven were meeting again so soon, but he was certainly glad to welcome them. The little oil lamp was lighted, and the shed looked warm and cosy.

The guy sat sedately in his chair while Peter collected a little more money. 'One pound fifty pence,' he announced. 'Jolly good. Now, who'd like to come and choose the fireworks with me tomorrow at dinner-time instead of waiting till Saturday? I thought three of us could go – and the rest can say now if there are any particular fireworks they'd like us to get.'

It was decided that George and Pam should go with Peter. Then Jack, grinning all over his face, told the Seven how he had done a bit of snooping on the Tiresome Three, and heard their threats of raiding the bonfire – and how he had told them they would find a bonfire laid on the top of Haylings Hill.

'And we went up there this morning, Peter and I, and put a silly little twig fire ready, with a note from the Secret Seven!' he said. 'I bet the Tiresome Three have taken a long walk up there after afternoon school today!'

'They'll be furious,' said Janet. 'I hope they won't come and raid *our* bonfire.'

'I don't think they know where it is at present,' said Jack. 'As soon as I hear that they do know – or are looking for it – I'll tell you. Then we can be on our guard.'

'Grrrrrr!' said Scamper, suddenly, and made them all jump.

'Can it be the Tiresome Three back from the hill *already*?' said Jack, startled. 'What's up, Scamper?'

'Grrrrrr!' said Scamper again, and all the hairs on his neck rose up. He ran to the door and listened intently.

Pam suddenly gave a loud shriek, and made everyone jump violently. Janet turned on her angrily. 'What did you scream like that for? That's just what the Tiresome Three want – to scare us and make us yell out!'

Pam pointed to the little shed window with a shaking finger. 'A face looked in there,' she said. 'I saw it.'

'Then it *is* Susie and her friends!' said Jack, fiercely. 'Why didn't we draw the curtain across?'

They all ran to the door and pulled it open, and Scamper ran out, barking. He sniffed all round, and then stood still, growling again.

'They've gone,' said Peter, shining his torch all round.

'Perhaps they came to raid the guy – take him away or something in revenge. Shut up, Scamper. There's nobody here now.'

They all went back and Peter drew the curtain across the window. 'Better break up the meeting now,' he said. 'Meet here on Saturday morning, please, and we'll finish building the bonfire. Jack, tell Susie we saw her – or one of the others – peering in. And tell her we hope they enjoyed their long walk!'

'I will,' said Jack, and cycled off. To his great astonishment he met Susie, Hilda and Doris at his front gate, walking wearily into the drive. Doris was almost in tears.

'You beast!' said Susie, angrily. 'Sending us all the way up there, to the top of Haylings Hill! That silly little bonfire – and the horrid note. Doris has hurt her ankle, falling on the hill – she could hardly get home. You're *mean*!'

'But – but wasn't it you, then, peering in at our shed window?' said Jack, amazed.

'I don't know what you're talking about,' said Susie. 'So don't try and be funny. I tell you, we've only just got back – and I'll have to see to poor Doris's ankle *at once*.'

They went round to the garden door, leaving Jack feeling puzzled – and rather sorry for his trick. He really hadn't meant anyone to fall down the hill.

But *who* had looked through the window? He had better telephone Peter immediately!

Fourteen

A dreadful shock

JACK telephoned Peter as soon as he had a chance. 'Peter? I say – it *wasn't* Susie or her friends who came and peeped in at our window tonight. They'd only just got back from Haylings Hill when I arrived home. Doris had hurt her ankle and was limping.'

Peter whistled. 'Who was it, then? Wait a minute, here's Dad. Dad – I say, Dad – you didn't peep in at our shed window tonight, did you?'

'No,' said his father. 'But the gardener was working late today – I expect he saw your light there, and peeped in.'

'Oh – so that was it,' said Peter, and told Jack. 'Anyway, the shed's locked,' he said. 'No one can get in. See you tomorrow, Jack.'

Susie was very, very angry about Jack's trick. 'I've a good mind to tell Mother,' she scolded. 'You should just *see* poor Doris's ankle. Well, you just look out for yourselves, you mean, horrible Seven. We're going to find your bonfire and pull it to bits! And if only we can get hold of your guy, we'll take him and burn him ourselves!'

'Don't be silly,' said Jack. 'The shed's locked, you know that. Yes, I know you found it unlocked the other night, but that was only for a few minutes while we went to get a chair for the guy. I tell you, I'm sorry about Doris's ankle. Now leave me in peace.'

But Susie wouldn't, and poor Jack had to retire to his bedroom. He wished once again that he and Peter hadn't played that trick on Susie and the others. Once Susie made up her mind to pay him out for anything, she usually did! Suppose she found their big bonfire? That would be the end of it!

Next day Peter, George and Pam went off to buy the fireworks. They managed to get all they wanted, except for some called Moon Rockets.

'They'll be in tomorrow morning,' said the shop-woman. 'You call for them then. And I'll have some in called "Catch-me-if-you-can" – little ones that rush about in the air, and hop all over the ground.'

'Oh, well will you keep some for us?' asked Peter. 'We've saved one pound fifty pence altogether – and we've spent just over a pound already. I'll keep the rest of the money and bring it in tomorrow for the other fireworks. I'd certainly like some of the Moon Rockets!'

He put down one pound and five pence in silver, and picked up the parcel of fireworks. George and Pam had helped to choose them and were very pleased. Peter put the rest of the money into his pocket.

'Forty-five pence,' he said. 'I'll make a note of what we've spent when I get back home, and put the change into the box on the shelf. If anyone has any more firework money they can add to it when we meet to make the bonfire bigger tomorrow morning. There's no meeting to-night.'

He popped into the shed when he got back, and put the money away safely. He took a look at the guy, and de-cided to ask his father for an old pipe. 'We didn't do anything about that,' he thought. 'And he *does* look as if a pipe would suit him!'

He asked his father later on in the evening. 'A pipe? Well, my old pipes are my favourite ones really,' said

his father. 'Still, wait a minute. I've got one with a broken stem. Your guy won't mind that, I'm sure.'

He found it and gave it to Peter. Scamper ran to the door and barked.

'Take him for a turn round the garden with you,' said Peter's mother.

'Right!' said Peter. 'Come on, Scamper – walkies! We'll take the pipe to the guy. Coming, Janet?'

'Got the key of the shed?' asked Janet. Peter fumbled in his pocket. Then he felt in his other pocket.

'Blow!' he said. 'Where is it? Gosh – surely I locked up the shed when I popped in with the money. Oh, *don't* say I left the key in the lock!'

'Quick – come and see,' said Janet, thinking at once of the Tiresome Three. They pulled on coats and tore down the garden to the shed, Scamper leaping about madly. They came to the door, and Peter shone his torch on the lock.

'Look – I *did* leave the key in it,' he said. 'What an absolute fathead I am! I really don't *deserve* to be the leader of the Secret Seven. Thank goodness Susie hasn't been along and taken it!'

He unlocked the door and they went into the shed, Peter holding the pipe for the guy. Janet gave a sudden yell and clutched his arm.

'Peter! *Peter!* Look at the guy! His clothes are gone! Susie *has* been here. Oh, why ever did you leave the key in the lock?'

Sure enough, the guy sat in his chair, wearing his mask and nothing else. He looked very foolish and fat as he sprawled there.

'The only thing the Tiresome Three have left him are the safety pins that pinned his trousers,' said Janet, tearfully. 'Oh Peter! Our lovely guy – the best one we've ever had! Whatever will the others say?'

Peter was simply horrified. To think that this was all his fault! He looked round the shed, hoping vainly to find the clothes thrown into a corner. But no – there wasn't even the cap to be seen.

'Come back to the house,' he said, dolefully, and locked the door carefully, putting the key into his pocket. 'This is simply awful. I'll get on to Jack straight away and tell him what the Tiresome Three have done.'

Jack was just as horrified as Peter and Janet, when he heard the news. He could hardly believe his ears.

'So *that's* where Susie and the others went this evening, is it?' he said. 'I thought they were having one of their silly meetings down in the summer-house, but they must have gone to our shed. My word – I'll go for Susie over this!'

He slammed down the receiver and went to find Susie. She and Hilda and Doris were sitting by the fire, reading. Jack exploded angrily, and pulled Susie's hair hard.

'What have you done with our guy's clothes? So *that's* where you disappeared to this evening – you went stealing!'

'Don't be funny,' said Susie, looking most astonished. 'We were up in the attic all evening, looking out jumble for Mother's sale.'

'You were *not*!' shouted Jack. 'Don't tell untruths. WHERE ARE THOSE CLOTHES?'

Fifteen
Oh, that Tiresome Three

Susie and Doris and Hilda looked quite alarmed when Jack shouted so loudly.

'I tell you,' began Susie, raising her voice too, 'I tell you *we* haven't got the clothes – but I'm jolly glad to hear your silly old guy has lost them. Ha ha!'

'Where did you hide the clothes?' shouted Jack again – and at that moment his mother put her head into the room.

'Jack! Stop shouting. What's the matter?'

'Susie and Doris and Hilda have taken the clothes off our guy,' blurted out Jack, forgetting that it was a mean trick to tell tales. But he did feel so very, very angry! 'And they are telling fibs about it. Oh yes you are, Susie, I know you!'

'That's enough,' said his mother. 'Go up to your room, Jack, and cool off. I'll speak to Susie.'

Jack stamped out of the room, boiling with rage. He looked into Susie's room, hoping to see the guy's clothes stuffed under the bed or in the wardrobe, but there was nothing there. He went into his own room and waited.

Soon his mother came in.

'You are not to say another word to Susie and her friends about that guy's clothes,' she said. 'You've upset the girls very much – and Susie told me how you and Peter tricked them into climbing all the way up Haylings Hill. I'm ashamed of you.'

'But, *Mother*,' said Jack, 'please listen. Mother, *please* ask Susie where she hid the guy's clothes.'

69

'I'm not going to discuss the subject at all,' said his mother, and shut the door. Jack sat and fumed. He didn't even dare to go down and telephone to Peter. He felt sure that the Tiresome Three would be giggling over his shoulder if he did.

The Seven had to meet at the shed the next morning – and it was a sad and sorry company! They gazed at their wonderful guy, now so bare and ugly, wearing only his mask, and Pam burst into tears.

'All the clothes I brought!' she sobbed. 'It's too bad! I think your mother ought to go to Susie's mother, Peter, and complain. It's *stealing*.'

'Well – not exactly,' said Jack, uncomfortably. 'I mean – I'm sure Susie will give them back after Bonfire Night, it's just one of her silly *tricks*. I was so angry last night I could have shaken her to bits!'

'It's all my fault, I'm afraid,' said Peter, humbly. 'If I hadn't left the key in the lock, it would never have happened. I take the whole blame. Susie just took her chance – it was a real bit of luck for her – just like when we left the door open to get the guy that chair. That was a bit of luck for her too.'

'Well – we'll have to try and get some more clothes,' said Colin. 'There's an old raincoat hanging in our garage. I'm sure nobody wants it. I'll get that. And somebody can surely get hold of another cap. The guy will just have to make do with those!'

'We bought the fireworks,' said Pam, changing the subject, very sorry for poor unhappy Peter. 'Fine ones! And we kept back forty-five pence to buy some of those new Moon Rockets. Shall I pop up to the shop and see if they're in, Peter?'

'Yes, do,' said Peter, taking the money-box from the

shelf. 'The money's here.' He shook the box, suddenly looking alarmed. He put it down quickly on the little table and took off the lid. Then he looked up, dismayed.

'The money's gone,' he said. 'Not a penny of it left. Forty-five pence all gone!'

There was a dead silence. Even Scamper did not move an ear. Then Jack spoke, his words falling over one another.

'If Susie took it, it was only a joke, Peter. Really, it was. She – she's not a thief.'

'Well, didn't she steal the guy's clothes?' demanded Barabara. 'I wouldn't put anything past the Tiresome Three!'

'No, no, wait,' said Peter. 'I feel like Jack – I don't believe Susie would ever *steal*. After all, she's Jack's sister. I think she and the others may have taken the clothes and the money to pay us out – meaning to keep them till after Bonfire Night and then give them back . . .'

'Yes – yes, that's what they'll do,' said Janet. I'm sure of it. Jack, just tell Susie you know they've got our money, but you jolly well want it back after Bonfire Night. We'll have to get the Moon Rockets then. We shouldn't have had such a feud on between us. It's getting too silly for words.'

'All right,' said Jack. 'And now for goodness sake let's go and collect wood for the bonfire. I can't sit here a moment longer. I feel too angry for words.'

They all got up and went out, Peter locking the door very carefully indeed. They walked rather silently to the field and looked at their bonfire.

'Someone's been digging round and about it,' said George. 'I wonder what for.' He stamped down the rough clods, and looked at the bonfire. 'It wants a good bit more

on!' he said. 'Cheer up, Jack, cheer up, Peter. You look as
if you've done a whole page of sums wrong!'

Even that joke didn't bring a smile to anyone's face.
What a blow to lose their guy's clothes *and* the rest of the
firework money! What a blow that Peter hadn't locked
the door last night!

They followed the same plan as before, collecting wood
and piling it at the edge of the wood, then roping it and
dragging it to the bonfire. It soon grew very big, and the
Seven began to feel more cheerful when they thought
what a blaze it would make. Scamper ran round with
twigs in his mouth, looking very busy indeed. He even
began to take them off the bonfire too, but that was soon
stopped!

'Look – look, there's Susie and the others!' said George,
suddenly. 'They must have been hunting about for our
bonfire.'

'*Where are our guy's clothes?*' yelled Pam, suddenly remembering how much trouble she had gone to in getting them.

'*We* haven't got them!' shouted back Susie.

'You have!' cried Pam. 'Don't you go near our bonfire. We know you'd take that away too, if you could.'

'Be quiet, Pam,' said Janet.

'We don't want a silly bonfire like this,' shouted Susie. 'Why, it'll fall to pieces if it's kicked. Look!'

And to the Seven's horror she and Hilda and Doris ran round it, kicking away some of the twigs. *Well!* Whatever next!

Sixteen

Keep guard on the bonfire!

As soon as the Seven ran across the field towards the bonfire, Susie and the others disappeared.

'You wait!' called Susie. 'We'll come back, and you won't find much of your bonfire left!'

'We'll just have to put someone on guard,' said Peter, dolefully. 'I'm beginning to think it was a great mistake to quarrel with Susie. She's too clever.'

They finished the bonfire, keeping a good look-out for the Tiresome Three, but not another sign of them did they see.

'Better take it in turns to watch the bonfire this afternoon,' said George.

'No. I know a better idea than that,' said Jack. '*I'll* watch Susie and the other girls. I won't let them out of my sight. And tonight I'll take them to the cinema, so that I know they'll not be up to mischief. Mother said she would give me the money for it. Mind you, I shan't *like* doing it, but it's the only sensible thing I can think of.'

'It's a very, very good idea,' said Janet. 'And it does mean we won't have to stand about in this cold field all day, watching the bonfire! Do you want Peter to keep you company tonight at the cinema? It would be rather awful for you to have those three girls all to yourself.'

'All right,' said Jack, gratefully. 'It would make things a bit easier.'

So that night Peter and Jack solemnly took the three giggling girls to the cinema. His mother was very pleased.

'I'm glad you've made up that silly quarrel,' she said to Jack. 'I knew the girls hadn't taken those clothes – it wouldn't be a bit like them to do a thing like that.'

Jack said nothing, but thought privately that it would be *exactly* like them. He had kept an eye on the three girls all the afternoon, and knew that they had not gone near the bonfire. And they would be safe under his wing at the cinema and until bedtime. That was something!

Next morning, which was Sunday, the three girls went to church, Jack with them. But in the afternoon Susie grew restive.

'Let's go for a walk,' she said to Hilda and Doris. Jack pricked up his ears at once. Ah – where to? The bonfire field?

'I'll go with you,' he said.

'No thanks,' said Susie. 'I don't particularly want to be under your eye any more. What do you think we are going to do? Kick your bonfire to pieces? I bet that's what you're thinking.'

As that was exactly what Jack *was* thinking, he couldn't help going red. And then, just at that moment, his father called him.

'Jack, old son, come and give me a hand with cleaning the car, will you?' he said.

'Er – well – I thought of going for a walk with the girls,' said poor Jack.

'*We* can spare him, Dad,' said Susie, with a wicked grin. 'So long, Jack. Be good!'

And away went the three girls, leaving Jack to go out to the garage and begin hosing the car. Blow! Now he couldn't possibly keep an eye on them. Wait – hadn't he better telephone Peter and tell him to guard the bonfire? It would be so awful to have such a beauty spoilt now!

'Can I go and telephone Peter, Dad?' he asked his father. 'I've – er – just remembered something important.'

'Well, wait till you've finished the hosing,' said his father. 'It can't be so terribly important that you have to go at once!'

So, for three-quarters of an hour Jack worked on the car, fuming. Suppose Susie and the others were ruining the bonfire now? How maddening it would be! He was very glad to rush off to the telephone as soon as his father gave him permission.

'Peter? Is that you? Listen, Susie and the others have gone out for a walk – but it's just *possible* they may go to the bonfire field. Keep an eye there this afternoon, will you?'

'Right,' said Peter. 'Thanks for phoning.' He called to Janet. 'Hey, Janet – that was Jack. He says Susie and her friends have gone out for a walk – will we keep an eye on the bonfire.'

'Oh my goodness – we'd better go out into the field straight away!' said Janet, and flew to get her coat. Peter fetched his and they went into the garden, and down to the bottom. In a few minutes they were out in the bonfire field.

No one was there. The field was empty. Probably Susie had taken her friends quite a different way! Peter glanced at the bonfire.

What a shock he got! He clutched Janet's hand and pointed to the bonfire, unable to say a word. There was very little of the huge pile to be seen. It had been scattered over a wide area. Big twigs, little twigs, branches – there they lay on the grass.

'They've destroyed it,' said Janet, and tears came to her

eyes. 'Oh, how *could* they? It was such a beauty too – so high and wide. Oh Peter – why didn't Jack telephone sooner? We could so easily have driven Susie away.'

Peter was very red in the face. He stared at the ruined bonfire, his mouth set and angry. 'Susie must have gone mad,' he said at last, and marched over to what was left of the great heap.

'What's this hole?' said Janet, in surprise, as they came up to where the bonfire had been built. 'It looks as if Susie and the others had a spade and scattered the wood everywhere and then dug a hole. Honestly, they must be mad! What are they up to, Peter?'

'I don't know,' said Peter, staring. 'Let's go and phone Jack. Wait a minute, though – surely that's Susie and her friends coming up the field? It *is*! let's go and tackle them – let's see what they've got to say! Come on!'

Seventeen

A spade – and a button!

Peter and Janet met the Tiresome Three as they drew near the bonfire. Suzie gazed at the ruined pile of wood in amazement.

'What's happened!' she said. 'Have you been kicking your bonfire about?'

'No – *you're* the ones who have done that,' said Peter, his voice trembling with anger.

'We've only just come!' said Doris, indignantly. 'You saw us!'

'So you say – but it's quite clear you've been here before,' said Peter. 'You're good at mean tricks, aren't you?'

Susie looked at him and then at the bonfire. 'Well, I won't say that we wouldn't have spoilt it a *bit*,' she said. 'But we wouldn't have destroyed it like this – and who dug that hole in the middle?'

'Don't pretend,' said Peter, in disgust. Janet suddenly tugged at his arm.

'Peter – Peter, they're *not* pretending! They're just as surprised as we are! Peter, it *wasn't* them!'

'Peter won't believe you,' said Susie, scornfully. 'Jack won't, either. Well, it just happens to be the truth, see – we've *only* – *just* – *come*! So what about looking round and finding out who really *did* do all this?'

Peter and Janet stared at her. She spoke very earnestly indeed.

'You think we took your guy clothes, and your money – and now you think we've ruined your bonfire. Well, we didn't. And that's the *truth*!'

And with that, Susie, Hilda and Doris marched off, heads in air, leaving Peter and Janet still staring, unable to say a word.

Janet found her tongue at last. She turned to Peter. 'Peter, they truly are not pretending. They certainly didn't ruin our bonfire – and I don't believe they did the other things either. Anyway, I never *could* believe that Susie took our money. It's someone else, Peter, *someone else* who is playing tricks!'

'But who?' said Peter, bewildered. 'And why steal the clothes off the guy? It seems such a mad thing to do.'

'Let's look round a bit,' said Janet. 'We might find footprints or something. And I wish I knew who had been digging about like this. It seems so *mad* somehow. Look at this big clod of earth thrown up. Do you suppose Burton knows anything about it? He knew we were making a bonfire, because we asked him for the hedge trimmings to burn.'

'Well, yes – Burton *might* have seen someone about!' said Peter. 'I wonder if he's around anywhere? He usually helps to milk the cows on Sunday, so that the cowman can get a bit of time off.'

'I think that's him over there,' said Janet looking in the direction of the wood. 'Perhaps he's going to his little hut. Let's go after him and ask him if he's seen anyone messing about in this field.'

They ran after the figure in the distance, but the man disappeared between the trees.

'Yes – I think it *is* Burton,' said Peter. 'Come on – I bet he's gone to his hut!'

They made their way into the wood till they came to the little overgrown hut. They called loudly. 'Burton! Burton! Are you there?'

There was no answer.

'I'm going inside,' said Peter, and disappeared through the half-open doorway. Janet followed him.

'No – he's not here,' said Peter, looking round. It was rather dark in the shed, but as his eyes grew used to the dimness, something caught his eye – something that glinted a little. He picked it up.

'A spade!' he said. 'And look, Janet – it's Burton's! It's got his name burnt across the handle. He always burns his name on his tools, in case they get stolen.'

Janet looked distressed. 'Peter! You don't think it could be *Burton* doing all these things, do you?' she said, anxiously. 'I like Burton. But – but – *someone's* been messing about round our bonfire with a spade – and this one's got Burton's name on it!'

'You mean it might have been Burton peering in at our window, and walking in when the door was unlocked and taking the guy clothes for himself?' said Peter. 'He certainly needs a few decent clothes! And taking our money too! But we've had Burton for *ages*, and Daddy thinks he's a wonder. It *can't* be old Burton – unless he's gone mad!'

'Well, this is certainly his spade,' said Janet. 'Oh, I can't *bear* it to be Burton! If we tell Daddy he'll lose his job.'

Peter looked round the hut again, puzzled and worried. It was bad enough to have thought that the Tiresome Three might have played mean tricks – but it was worse still to think of old Burton doing such peculiar things!

He saw something small and round lying on the floor, and picked it up.

'A button,' he said. 'Look, Janet — it seems familiar, somehow. Do you recognize it?'

Yes, Janet did! 'Of *course*, don't you remember? The guy's old tweed coat had buttons like this — half-yellow and half-brown! The thief has been here — sat down here — and a button fell off the coat. I expect he was wearing it. Peter, who in the world is it? That coat's too big for Burton, surely.'

'He *could* have had it altered,' said Peter. 'Come on — let's go home. There's something queer about all this.'

Eighteen

Jack has a sudden idea

PETER and Janet went home feeling rather upset and extremely puzzled.

'Better tell all the others tomorrow at school what has happened,' said Peter. 'If they could each bring something to eat, and Mother would let us have lemonade again, we could have a quick tea, and then go out and rebuild the bonfire. We've got the guy all right, and we've got fireworks – not as many as we hoped, but still, enough to have a bit of fun.'

'Yes, it's disappointing that our grand plan for a wonderful guy and lashings of fireworks has been spoilt – but we'll just have to make do with second best,' said Janet.

So, after afternoon school on Monday, the Seven met once again in the shed, with Scamper to welcome them as usual. The girls had been told by Janet at school what had happened the day before, and the boys had been told by Peter. They sat down, opened their bags of cakes and biscuits, and accepted lemonade from Peter.

'Well,' began Peter, 'you know more or less what happened to our bonfire yesterday – *ab*solutely ruined – and you know that Janet and I think it wasn't Susie and her friends after all.'

'You said it was probably Burton, the old hedger-and-ditcher,' said Colin.

'Well, it wasn't,' said Peter, and this was news to everyone but Janet. 'My father happened to mention him this morning, and said he had been ill for some days and in bed. So it certainly *wasn't* him.'

'Probably some tramp then, who peered into our shed, saw the nice warm clothes the guy was wearing, and stole them – and the money too,' said Jack. 'But what *I* can't understand is, who ruined our bonfire – and what's the sense of making holes round it?'

There was a silence – and then, quite suddenly Jack smacked his hand down so hard on his knee that everyone jumped almost out of their skin.

'We're blind!' said Jack. 'We're idiots! We're complete fatheads!'

The others stared at him in alarm. Whatever did he mean!

'Hold on, Jack, old thing,' said Peter. 'What's up? You look as if you've seen a ghost or something!'

'Well, I haven't. But I think I've spotted the person who's been stealing our things and spoiling our plans!' said Jack. 'Of course, of course, of *course*!'

'Who is it?' demanded Peter.

'Well, who could it be but the third thief who escaped when the other two were caught – the ones who robbed Colin's Granny!' said Jack. 'Don't you *see*?'

'The third thief – but . . .' began Peter.

'Yes! He knew the police had a full description of him, it said so in the papers! So he had to get other clothes – *and he got them from our guy*!' said Jack.

'Of course! Don't you remember, he was tall and fat!' said Janet. 'He'd need big clothes – and he must have spotted them on our guy . . .'

'Yes – that time he peeped in at our window!' half shouted George. 'It wasn't the gardener or Burton, it must have been that thief!'

'He needed money – and took ours!' said Barbara.

'And do you know what I think? I bet the other two

thieves buried the stolen valuables in our field!' cried
Peter. 'And that's what all the digging's for – those holes –
those thrown-up clods! He stole Burton's spade for
that!'

'And since Burton's been ill, the thief must have been
sleeping in his old hut!' put in Pam. 'And that's how that
button came there – he was wearing the guy's coat and it
came off.'

Scamper felt the excitement round him and began to
bark, wagging his tail hard. Peter patted him.

'Quiet, Scamper, quiet. You shall join in the excitement in a minute. Listen, all of you. That thief is still
somewhere in the woods – maybe in Burton's hut this very
minute. I don't believe he has found those hidden valuables – and he won't leave till he does. Well then . . .'

'Well, then, we'd better tell the *police* what we think!'
cried Jack. 'Or he may find the hidden goods and disappear. Aren't we idiots not to have thought of it before? All
that fuss and excitement over that robbery – and here
we've had the third robber hanging about our shed for
ages!'

'And we thought it was poor Susie,' said Janet. 'Honestly, I feel awful about that.'

'Look – don't forget it's Bonfire Night,' said Barbara.
'Telephone the police straight away, or we'll never have
time to rebuild our bonfire, take the guy out and let off the
fireworks. *Please* don't let's spoil Bonfire Night.'

'All right, all right,' said Peter. 'I'll go and tell the
police what we think – though they may not believe it, of
course. Jack, you and George take out the guy. Pam,
you're responsible for the fireworks. Janet, remember the
matches for the bonfire. Colin and Barbara, start re-
building it as quickly as you can!'

'Right, Captain!' said Jack. 'Scamper – lead the way!'

'And for goodness sake look out for the thief!' shouted Peter, as he ran out of the shed door to go in and telephone. 'I bet he's still about somewhere!'

Nineteen

Quite a lot happens

EVERYONE obeyed orders, and very soon the guy, in his old raincoat and cap, was being carried out of the shed in his chair, and down the garden into the field. Pam followed, hugging the big parcel of fireworks. Janet raced up to the house for a box of matches.

Soon they were all in the field. It was getting dark now, and they would have to use their torches before long.

'Blow!' said Jack, feeling a few spots of rain on his face. 'I believe it's going to rain!'

Colin and Barbara set to work to build up the scattered bonfire heap. It wasn't very easy in the half-darkness. Jack and George helped too, once they had set down the guy.

Colin suddenly pulled Janet's coat. 'I say,' he said, in a whisper. 'Look – is that someone over there – on the other side of the field?'

Janet looked – and what she saw made her nudge Jack and George. 'Be very quiet!' she said, in a low voice. 'Look over there!'

They all looked across the misty, rainy field, and saw what Colin had seen . . . a man, digging, digging, digging! He hadn't seen them away in the distance, for he had his back to them.

'The third robber!' whispered Janet. 'What do we do now?'

'Take no notice at all,' said Colin. 'Just keep him under our eye till the police come. That's about all we can do.'

'Can you see if he's dressed in our guy's old clothes?' whispered Pam.

'No – it's too misty now, and he's just too far away,' said Colin. 'But it *must* be the thief – else why is he digging? Come on. Build up the bonfire. Stick the guy on top. Pretend we're going about our own business and haven't even noticed him.'

So they all rebuilt the bonfire at top speed, and then, with a great heave, set the guy and his chair firmly on top.

'He's sitting there beautifully,' said Jack. 'Firm as anything. Blow this rain – I don't believe our bonfire will light up at all. Everything's getting soaked.'

'I think it's terribly disappointing,' said Pam. 'Every single thing's gone wrong with our wonderful bonfire plans! Everything!'

'Shut up – the fellow's coming across the field,' said Colin, in a low voice. 'Don't be afraid – we've got Scamper. Get on with the bonfire, and talk, and don't take any notice.'

The man was now almost up to them. Pam glanced round and gave a little cry, which she choked in her throat – he was wearing the trousers, the tweed coat, the rubber boots and the cap in which their guy had first been dressed! Scamper had now begun to bark and growl. The man spoke roughly.

'Clear out of this field. It belongs to the farmer. You're not allowed to have bonfires here.'

'My father is the farmer it belongs to,' said Janet. 'He knows we are building it here. Please be careful of our dog. He bites.'

The man lifted his spade as Scamper jumped round him, barking, and the children all yelled at once.

'Don't you hit him!'

'Stop that!'

'Put that spade down, don't hit the dog!'

'Scamper, come here!'

What would have happened next nobody knew – for quite suddenly two cars drew up on the road side of the field, and six dark figures leapt out.

'The police!' shouted Jack, excited. 'Look – they've come already!'

In a trice the man was off in the rainy mist, with Scamper at his heels and the six children after him. He kicked out at the dog and struck him on the leg. Scamper yelped and came limping back to Janet.

'Here's the man, somewhere over here!' shouted Jack, waving his torch. The dark figures fanned out and came across the field. Then suddenly someone ran panting up to them from behind – and it was Peter, who, after telephoning the police, had stopped to tell everything to his mother, and had then raced down to the field to join the others.

'My word – the police have been quick!' he said. 'They believed my story – every word of it! Did I hear you say the man was here in the field?'

'Yes – Scamper went after him and so did we,' said Jack. 'But he kicked him and hurt him. Watch out for the man – but let's keep together. The fellow ran off over in that direction. He's sure to be caught, the police are all round the field.'

Scamper limped off, barking. *He* had caught sight of the man. It was maddening for the Seven to stand in the half-darkness, and hear shouts, and the sounds of running footsteps, and not be able to see a thing in the rain that was now pouring down.

Scamper gave a yelp as if he was in pain, and the Seven ran to him. Peter felt his leg anxiously. 'I don't *think* it's broken!' he said.

A policeman came up. 'Did you see that fellow on this side of the field?' he said. 'I'm afraid we've lost him in this rain. Good gracious – whatever's that thing right over there?'

'It's our bonfire,' said Peter. 'And the poor old guy's sitting on top, waiting to be burnt – but he'll be so wet through we'll have to give up all idea of it, I'm afraid.'

'Gave me quite a turn, seeing the guy up there on that heap,' said the policeman. 'Well – I'm afraid we'll have to give up the chase. The man may have slipped into the wood – we'll never get him there.'

The Seven heard the policemen gathering together, and then by the light of their torches making for the two police cars.

'Blow!' said Peter. 'Now that fellow won't be caught. He may be a mile away by now.'

'He's not,' said Janet, suddenly, right in his ear, in a voice shaking with excitement. 'He's not! Peter – he's sit-up there on our bonfire! He's got the guy's raincoat on – but I saw his rubber boots in the light of my torch. *That's* where he's hiding, Peter! He knew we wouldn't light the bonfire in this rain!'

Peter let out a long breath of amazement, and walked over to the bonfire. Yes – Janet was right! What a hiding-place! There sat the thief, in the guy's chair, the raincoat over his clothes, the mask on his face – on the top of the bonfire! Thrown down behind was the real guy, robbed of his coat and mask.

'Stay here and fiddle about round the bonfire,' Peter said in a low voice to the others. 'I'll take Scamper in case he smells the man up there and barks – and I'll try and catch the police before they drive off. Stay here now, while I rush across the field.'

Twenty

Bang! Crash! Whoosh!

PETER tore right across the field. He shouted as he came near the cars, and waved his torch. One car was just driving off, but stopped.

'We've got the man!' he shouted. 'He's sitting on top of our bonfire, dressed in the guy's raincoat and mask, but we saw his boots. Come quickly.'

Everything then happened very, very suddenly. The police raced across the field, the man leapt off the bonfire, Scamper limped on three legs to stop him – and over went the thief! Before he could get up, he was caught! He began to shout and struggle.

'You go back home, you kids,' said the sergeant. 'You'll get soaked. Sorry your bonfire night's been spoilt – you'd better have it tomorrow! We'll be digging up this field in the morning, and maybe we'll get the buried goods before you light your bonfire! We'll come and dance round it if we do!'

The Seven watched the policemen disappear through the rain, the prisoner held tightly. Janet gave an enormous sigh.

'I suddenly feel dreadfully tired,' she said. 'Let's go in. I'm soaked.'

'Well, it was very exciting, but not much of a bonfire night – especially after all our wonderful plans,' said Jack.

'And poor Scamper's hurt,' said Peter. 'I don't feel like having a bonfire night at all, now. Let's give up the idea –

and not bother about it tomorrow. After all, we've not got
an enormous lot of fireworks – and our bonfire's soaked –
and so is our guy. Come on in.'

But next morning they all felt very differently! The
sergeant telephoned to say that they could have the third
robber's guy clothes if they wanted them – they had found
the man's own clothes. 'And I have another little surprise
for you,' he said.

'What?' asked Peter.

'Well – I'm very pleased with your help,' said the sergeant. 'And I am sending along a bumper box of fireworks,
with my best thanks. Enough for about twenty of you!
Have a good time tonight!'

'Oh – thanks a lot!' said Peter, thrilled.

All the others were delighted too, when they heard, and
great plans were made after morning school.

'My mother says you are all to come at five and she'll
give us a smashing tea – and Dad will come out and set the
bonfire going with us,' said Peter.

'And Burton's coming back today and says he'll build the bonfire sky-high,' said Janet. 'The other wood is soaked through. He'll bring some dry branches from the wood-shed.'

'There's just one thing more,' said Peter. 'Jack I feel *awful* about Susie. Simply awful. I mean – we accused her and the others of – of –'

'Go on – say it – of stealing!' said Jack. 'Well – *they* didn't have any fireworks last night either – I expect you'd like them to come to our show tonight, wouldn't you?'

'Yes. Yes, we'd *all* like them to,' said Peter. 'But do you think Susie will *want* to come? After all, we were pretty beastly in the things we said.'

'Let's write her a note from everyone of us,' said Janet. So between them they wrote a note, and Jack gave it to Susie. She looked most astonished and opened it at once.

'*Dear Susie,*' she read,

First of all we're very sorry for all the awful things we said. We really are. We would be awfully glad if you and Hilda and Doris would come to our firework party to-night. We've been sent the biggest box of fireworks you ever saw. Please do come and help us to set them off. Come to tea in the shed first. The password is Wee Willie Winkie.

With many apologies to you from

The Secret Seven.'

'Gracious goodness!' said Susie, her eyes shining. 'Wait till Hilda and Doris see this! Come to your *party*? I should jolly well think we will! And I *say* – does it really mean that we can meet in the shed with you – and say the password?'

'Yes – but only just this *once*,' said Jack. 'And please do behave yourself, Susie, and tell Hilda and Doris to as well.'

'Oh, I *will*,' said Susie. 'My word – *what* a surprise!'

And so, for the first time, Susie actually said the password and was admitted to the Secret Seven shed with Hilda and Doris. Not to a *meeting*, though – just to a tea-party. She was really very nice, for she waved away everyone's apologies, and smiled round in delight.

'Don't apologize! I've said just as awful things as you did, and done them too! We did our best to spoil your bonfire night – though that thief did far more than we did! And thanks *most* awfully for letting us come here and say the password. I never, *never* thought you'd do that.'

Everyone warmed to the generous-natured Susie, and Janet began to wonder however they could have thought such dreadful things of her and the others. 'But oh dear – I wouldn't be surprised if Susie's nice behaviour doesn't last very long,' she thought. 'Or ours either, come to that! So we must make the best of tonight!'

They certainly did. Come out to the field and listen.

BANG! CRASH! WHIZZZZZZZZZ! Whooooosh-ee-whoooosh-eewhooosh! *That* was the first Moon Rocket!

Sizzle-sizzle-sizzle – the bonfire is burning high – what a sight the flames are! And there's the old guy, plump and wobbly, dressed in coat, trousers, boots and cap, sitting high on top. Bang! A rocket flew by his ear, and made him jerk his head.

'He's laughing! The old guy's laughing!' shouted Janet, dancing round the bonfire. 'He says he's as warm as toast at last!'

BANG! Good-bye, Secret Seven, see you again soon! WHOOOOOOOSH! Look out, Peter, that rocket went very near your nose! CRASH! What in the wide world was *that*?

Only one figure is missing from the Grand Firework Party. Guess who it is? Yes, it's dear old Scamper. He's terrified of bangs and crashes, so he is lying comfortably in his basket by the fire, pretending that he can't go because his leg is bandaged!

Good-bye, Scamper! Give the Secret Seven a lick from us when next you see them!